Little Hippo® Books

145 Pinelawn Road, Melville, New York 11747
Licensed exclusively to Imagine That Group Ltd
Text copyright © 2011 Seema Barker
Illustration copyright © 2011 Imagine That Group Ltd
All rights reserved
0 2 4 6 8 9 7 5 3 1
Manufactured in Zhejiang, China

Written by Seema Barker
Illustrated by Kirsten Richards

ISBN 978-1-78700-757-4

The Tangle Fairy

Written by Seema Barker

For my gorgeous girls Jaya, Tara, Aasha—love Mummyji (SB)

Whilst brushing her hair
Jaya wanted to know,
"Why don't the knots in
my hair seem to go?
Each bedtime we brush
it, it's smooth and long.
But when I wake up it's
frizzy and wrong!"

"When kids
fall asleep," her
mommy replied,
"a Tangle Fairy
visits each child."
Jaya felt confused,
it sounded quite scary.
She needed to talk to
the bad Tangle Fairy.

"Hello Tangle Fairy."
(Jaya jumped out
of bed, to make sure
the wand wasn't too
near her head.)

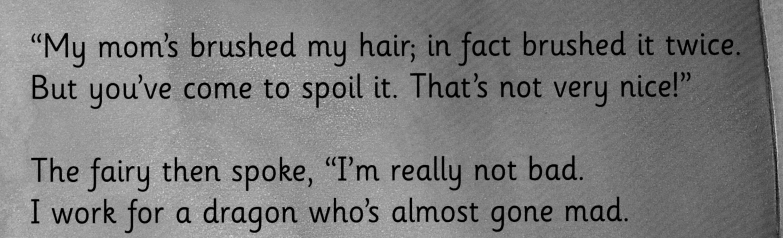

"My mom's brushed my hair; in fact brushed it twice.
But you've come to spoil it. That's not very nice!"

The fairy then spoke, "I'm really not bad.
I work for a dragon who's almost gone mad.
She's fearsome and fiery. She's red, blue and green.
And she's got the sharpest teeth you've ever seen."

Jaya was puzzled, "I believe what you've said.
But why would a dragon want knots on my head?"
"Her name is Glenda, she lives in Wales.
She's ever so angry because
she's got scales."

"I've seen her quite often, just pacing her lair,
while dreaming of having long, beautiful hair."

"She's so full of envy
she just doesn't care.
She makes me upset you
with mad, tangly hair!"

Jaya thought that was silly and started to laugh.
The dragon just needed her own headscarf.
"When my aunt was sick her hair all fell out.
She now wears headscarves when
she's out and about."

"Now that's an idea," the fairy
then said. "I'll make her a scarf
from the sheet of your bed."

The next day Jaya spluttered, "Hey this isn't fun!"
When she saw she had tangles despite what she'd done.
Again Jaya waited. Would the fairy be nice,
when Jaya asked her why she'd ignored her advice?

"Oh dear," fairy said, "I'm really not bad.
I work for a witch who's almost gone mad.
She's ugly and toothy, she scares cats and dogs.
She loves turning princes
into small frogs!"

"In Scotland she lives, her name is McGrace,
and her hair is simply all over the place.
She's cut it, she's washed it, she's even used glue.
She's cast spells and magic but nothing will do."

"She's so full of envy, she just doesn't care.
She makes me upset you with
mad, tangly hair!"

THE BEST
SPELLS
BOOK
EVER!

STEP-BY-STEP SPELLS

QUICK SPELLS

THE BEST
SPELLS BOOK EVER! VOL. 2

WITCHES HANDBOOK

THE ULTIMATE SPELL BOOK

THE BEST
SPELLS BOOK EVER! VOL. 3

ADVANCED WITCHCRAFT

Jaya knew just how the witch could solve that.
It wasn't that hard; simply put on a hat.
"When Grandma goes walking, her hair blows around.
She puts on a hat which soon calms it down."

"Now that's an idea," the fairy said back.
"I'll make her a hat that's pointy and black."

Next day Jaya screamed and counted to ten,
when she saw she had lots of tangles again.
She questioned the fairy, who then replied,
"I'm really not bad. There's no witch or
dragon, there's no one that's mad."

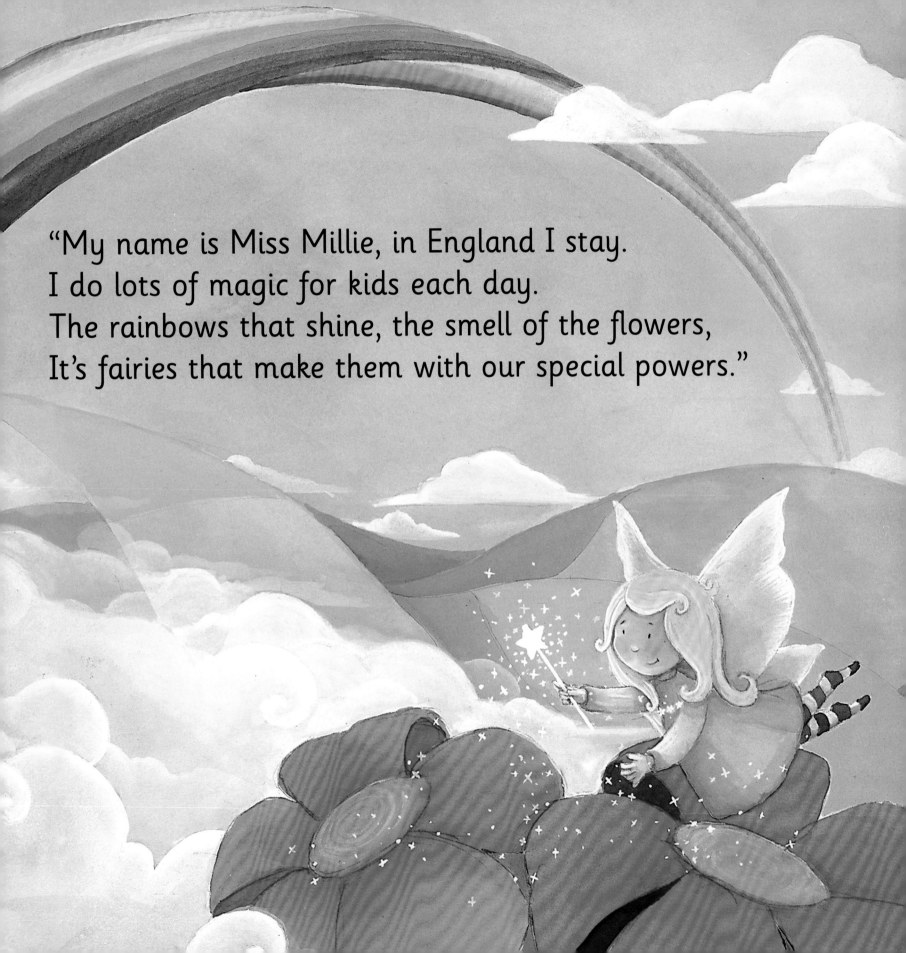

"My name is Miss Millie, in England I stay.
I do lots of magic for kids each day.
The rainbows that shine, the smell of the flowers,
It's fairies that make them with our special powers."

Jaya looked puzzled,
"I believe what you've said.
But why would a fairy
want knots on my head?"
"We work all day long,"
sighed fairy Miss Millie.
"But sometimes I really
just want to be silly."

"So that's why I come here,
it may sound unfair.
I'm just having fun putting
knots in your hair!"

That made Jaya laugh so much she could shout. (As she really loves just messing about.)

Like when she puts socks on her hands, not her feet,

or hides from her sisters whilst under a sheet.

Sometimes she puts
stickers all over
Mom's shoes,

and when Daddy comes
home she jumps out
and shouts BOO!

She jumps in big puddles,
it really feels great.
Though Mommy says not to,
sometimes Jaya can't wait!

So Jaya said, "Come put knots in my hair.
If you're having fun, then I really don't care."
The fairy then smiled, the bright moonlight
shone, she blew out a kiss and then…

...she was gone!